Miriam Moss was born in Aldershot, in Hampshire, and has lived
in the Middle East, Africa and China. In 1977 she took a combined degree
in Education and English, and went on to work as a teacher in the U.K. and
Kenya before beginning her writing career. She has written over 50 non-fiction titles,
and turned to writing fiction several years ago. Her most recent books include
Jigsaw (Templar), *Henry's Kite,* and *Windswept* (both for Hazar).
She lives in Lewes, Sussex.

Adrienne Kennaway was born in New Zealand and studied at Ealing Art School and
the Accademia de Belle Arte in Rome. She enjoys painting animals, and learned
how to scuba dive in order to be able to paint tropical marine fish. Her previous titles
include *Crafty Chameleon* (Winner of the 1987 Kate Greenaway Medal),
Hot Hippo and *Awkward Aardvark* (all Hodder & Stoughton),
and *Rainbow Bird* (Frances Lincoln).

For my mother ✳ M.M.
For Jeff ✳ A.K.

Arctic Song copyright © Frances Lincoln Limited 1999
Text copyright © Miriam Moss 1999
Illustrations copyright © Adrienne Kennaway 1999

The right of Miriam Moss to be identified as the Author of this Work
and Adrienne Kennaway as the Illustrator of this Work has been asserted
by them in accordance with the Copyright, Designs and Patents Act, 1988.

First published in Great Britain in 1999 by
Frances Lincoln Limited, 4 Torriano Mews
Torriano Avenue, London NW5 2RZ

First paperback edition 2000

British Library Cataloguing in Publication Date
available on request

ISBN 0-7112-1326-7 hardback
0-7112-1305-4 paperback

Set in Palatino
Printed in Hong Kong

3 5 7 9 8 6 4 2

ARCTIC SONG

MIRIAM MOSS

Illustrated by

ADRIENNE KENNAWAY

FRANCES LINCOLN

There is a land of frozen darkness,
lost in ice and snow.
Every year, for a short time,
the sun visits
and the land of midnight
becomes the land of the midnight sun.

One morning, a mother polar bear
breaks through the snow roof of her den.
Her cubs follow,
stretching and blinking in the light.

The mother sniffs the air,
rolls over and over in the powdery snow
and slides down the hill on her back.

The cubs pounce and play,
then skid down to the mint-green sea
to dabble their paws
and scratch designs on ice.

An inky raven looks for trouble.
He spies the cubs and flaps down.
With flashing feathers
and beady eye,
he weaves mischievous stories
about the magic
of whalesong.

The cubs are bewitched.

Sensing danger
their mother turns,
arrows her wedge-shaped head
and runs hissing, shooing the raven off.

Too late.
The cubs are curious.
"When can we hear whalesong, Mother?"
"When you are older," she says.
"Singing whales live far away. Too far."

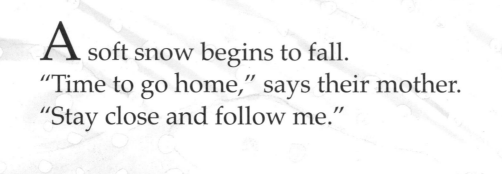

A soft snow begins to fall.
"Time to go home," says their mother.
"Stay close and follow me."

But the cubs hang back
until their mother
disappears into the haze.

Then they scamper off
to search for whalesong.

The cubs race through the snow
until small rocks and stones
break the whiteness.

The sun outlines a herd of caribou
tramping northwards
in raggedy lines.
The last caribou chips at the snow crust
with her hoof.
"Where can we hear whalesong?"
"I do not know," says the caribou.

With dark mountains behind them
and snow geese overhead,
the cubs pad on.
Before them a giant rock
turns into a great bearded musk ox.
The wind lifts and blows its shaggy hair
like curtains.
"Where can we hear whalesong?"
"I do not know," says the musk ox.

The cubs dance in buzzing meadows
threaded with silver streams
and carpeted with flowers.
Then, yawning,
they roll on beds of moss
and listen
to the arctic loon's haunting cry.

A friendly fox trips by.
"Where can we hear whalesong?"
"The sea. Not far. That way."
She points.

The cubs splash through ice pools,
and, at the jagged ocean edge,
they watch monstrous icebergs,
shaped like castles,
drip in the midnight sun.

A walrus lolls on floating flat ice.
"Where can we hear whalesong?"
"Walrus song sounds better," he says, "listen."
On the stony bottom of the shallow sea
he plays his drumbeat song.
"Thank you," say the cubs,
"but we want to hear whalesong too."

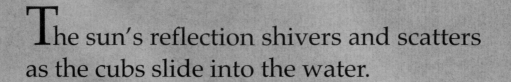

The sun's reflection shivers and scatters
as the cubs slide into the water.

Nearby a narwhal points its spiralled tusk
at the clouds.
"Can you sing whalesong?" call the cubs.
"Dive deeper, dive deeper," says the narwhal.

With ivory coats smooth as silk,
the cubs plunge deep
into an underwater world
lit by the silvery flash of fish.

Above them
a bowhead whale shoulders through the water,
her calf alongside,
her long, curved smile full of stiffly fringed hair.
She rises to let out a deep, deep blow, dives
and starts to sing
whalesong,
her song,
a mother singing to her young.

"Time to go home," the song sings,
"before winter comes and darkness falls."

The cubs listen, spellbound.
For inside the song
they hear their mother calling,
see her searching,
feel her waiting.

The cubs turn
and swim homewards,
shoulder to shoulder.

They climb on to land,
their coats running heavily
with jade green droplets.

A stormy sky threatens.
A bitter wind bites deep.
Loose-limbed, they run across the ice,
snow flying from coats and paws.

At dusk they reach their den.
"Mother," they call, "we heard whalesong!"
A paw appears, then a head.

Seeing them, their mother's eyes light up.
Darkness falls,
and the snow shuffles softly again
over the roof of the warm den.

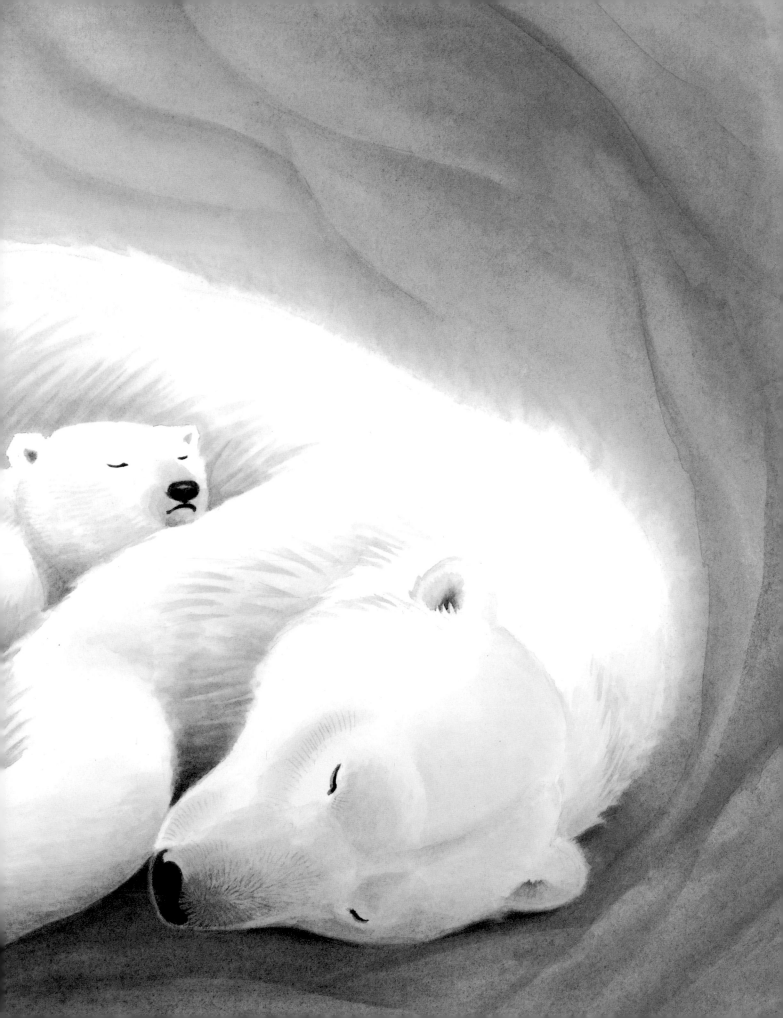

About the Arctic

The Arctic is an area of cold seas and cold lands surrounding the North Pole. During the Arctic winter the sun does not rise. Light comes from the moon and stars, reflecting off ice and snow. In summer, the sun is above the horizon for long periods, but the Arctic is never warm. There are no trees. The plants are all small and slow-growing, and many have brilliantly-coloured flowers.

There are few land animals in the Arctic. The shaggy *musk ox* is smaller than an ordinary cow, but its coat is long and thick. Smaller still is the *caribou*, (also known as a reindeer). *Polar bears*, by contrast, are very big and strong. They are powerful swimmers, at home both on land and in the sea. A layer of fat beneath the skin helps keep them warm in the icy waters. Polar bear mothers are devoted to their cubs, playing with them and protecting them from harm. When food is scarce, the mother is careful to divide it so that each cub gets its fair share.

An *Arctic fox* is about a third as long as a polar bear from nose to tail, but the bear is almost a hundred times heavier. There are two types of Arctic fox: one has a white winter coat and a brown summer coat, and the other changes from pale winter grey to darker grey in summer.

Few birds spend all year in the Arctic, but huge numbers fly north to enjoy the long daylight hours, returning south when their young are able to fly with them.

Arctic waters are home to *walrus, seals, narwhals* and other whales, fish and many smaller creatures. The whales whose songs are most familiar to humans through television and sound recordings are the humpback whales, but the *bowhead whale* has its own voice. Bowhead whales live only in the colder waters, and rarely travel far from the ice. They make various noises, among them a loud 'Hmmmm', sometimes rising, sometimes falling, through the northern seas.

OTHER PICTURE BOOKS IN PAPERBACK
FROM FRANCES LINCOLN

RAINBOW BIRD
Eric Maddern
Illustrated by Adrienne Kennaway

"I'm boss for Fire," growls rough, tough Crocodile Man, and he keeps the
rest of the world cold and dark, until one day clever Bird Woman sees her
opportunity and seizes it. An Aboriginal fire myth, lit with glowing illustrations.

Suitable for National Curriculum English - Reading, Key Stage 1
Scottish Guidelines English Language - Reading, Levels A and B

ISBN 0-7112-0898-0

CURIOUS CLOWNFISH
Eric Maddern
Illustrated by Adrienne Kennaway

When little Clownfish decides to explore, she discovers just how dangerous a
coral pool can be. A tropical underwater world, beautifully illustrated by
Kate Greenaway Medal winner, Adrienne Kennaway.
"Children will learn a lot about the many creatures on a coral reef,
both from the detailed, accurate illustrations and the simple storyline." *Child Education*

Suitable for National Curriculum English - Reading, Key Stage 1
Scottish Guidelines English Language - Reading, Levels A and B;
Environmental Studies, Levels A and B

ISBN 0-7112-0757-7

TOMS' RABBIT
A True Story from Scott's Last Voyage
Meredith Hooper
Illustrated by Bert Kitchen

It's Christmas day in the Antarctic, and Tom the Sailor is looking for a safe, cosy
place on board ship for his pet rabbit to make her nest. At last he settles her in the hay,
where she gives birth to 17 babies. An unusual picture book based on diaries by men
from Scott's second expedition in search of the South Pole.

Suitable for National Curriculum English - Reading, Key Stage 1;
History, Key Stage 1 and Geography, Key Stage 1
Scottish Guidelines English Language - Reading, Levels A and B;
Environmental Studies, Levels A and B

ISBN 0-7112-1184-1

Frances Lincoln titles are available from all good bookshops.
Prices are correct at time of publication, but may be subject to change.